Disney's Aladdin

THE MAGIC CARPET'S SECRET

by Joanne Barkan

Illustrations by
Brooks Campbell and Kenny Thompkins

ISBN 1-56326-255-X

CHAPTER 1

"Come on, Carpet! Fly!" said Aladdin.

"Try again, Carpet. Please, just once more!" Jasmine pleaded.

The edge of the Magic Carpet rippled. A tassel fluttered, then the Carpet lay still on the floor of the throne room.

"Poor thing!" Jasmine sighed. "It can't fly at all."

Aladdin's pet monkey, Abu, patted the Carpet gently and sniffled.

"This is hard for all of us, Abu. Here," said Jasmine, handing him a handkerchief.

Abu blew his nose hard.

Aladdin paced back and forth. "We can't

let this happen," he said. "I don't care if it takes until the north wind blows south—we're going to save my magic carpet!"

Great gusts of wind swept through the open windows. The air swirled into an immense spiral. As it spun faster, the spiral turned white, then lavender, then bright blue.

"Genie!" shouted Jasmine.

Aladdin and the Genie had first met when Aladdin was a beggar on the streets of Agrabah. The Genie of the Lamp had granted Aladdin three wishes. When Aladdin used his third wish to set the Genie free, they had become the best of friends.

The blue spiral stopped twirling.

"Well, howdy doo! How are things? Feeling good? Not so good? Have I got a deal for you!"

The Genie towered over them. He was wearing brand-new workout clothes.

"You're looking pale, worried, out-of-sorts—UNHEALTHY! And what's with that carpet? It looks downright sicko!"

"It is sick," said Jasmine. "Genie, we need your help. A month ago, the Carpet began

losing its power to fly—"

"Not to worry," said the Genie. "I've got an A-plus cure—the Alhambra Health Spa! Great oasis setting, four-star, low-cal restaurant, exercise classes three times a day. We'll get that lazy-bones carpet flipping around again. Grab your bathing suits. We're on our way!"

"But, Genie," said Aladdin, "we can't go anywhere. The Carpet is sick."

"What do you expect?" the Genie said. "Look at how you live! Rich foods, lounging around this palace all day—yuck!"

"It has nothing to do with us," said Aladdin. "Slow down for a minute. We need your help."

"Slow down? Are you kidding? Jazz aerobics starts in fifteen minutes. I've got to check into the hotel, weigh in at the fitness center, and talk to the dietician about my allergies. I'm late!"

The Genie began twirling furiously and spiraled away.

"Now what?" muttered Aladdin. He stared

at the Carpet.

Abu sniffled again and blew his nose.

"At least we can try to make it comfortable," said Jasmine. She knelt down and ran her hands over the blue and purple weaving. One corner of the Carpet lifted off the floor. The gold tassel twisted itself into a slender point. It touched the floor with short, choppy movements.

"It's trying to fly," Jasmine murmured. The tassel shook itself. It began touching the floor again. Jasmine watched closely.

"Aladdin!" she called. "Come quickly!" Aladdin and Abu raced to where Jasmine was kneeling next to the Carpet.

"The Carpet is trying to tell us something!" she said.

"It's just trying to move," said Aladdin.

"No, it's tracing letters on the floor," said Jasmine. "It's spelling out a word!"

The tassel paused and then started moving again. One long stroke. Two shorter strokes.

"It looks like the letter K!" said Aladdin.

Jasmine nodded. The tassel began again. A

long stroke. A short stroke. A long stroke.

"H," said Jasmine.

The tassel touched the floor again. A deep curve like a horseshoe.

"U," said Aladdin.

The tassel trembled and sank to the floor.

"Try to go on," said Aladdin. "Please."

Jasmine lifted the tassel so that most of it rested on her palm. Just the tip touched the floor. It made one long stroke, a small curve, and a short stroke.

"R!" said Aladdin. "Carpet, don't stop!"

Quivering, the tassel rose. It wavered in the air, but then lurched forward and collapsed on the floor.

laddin and Jasmine patted the Carpet and smoothed its nap, but it could no longer move.

"K-H-U-R..." Aladdin said. "What could it mean? It's not a word I've ever heard."

"I have no idea," said Jasmine. "How about you, Abu?"

Abu shook his head.

"Well," said Aladdin, "it has something to do with a carpet. So maybe we should consult a carpet expert. There's a man in the market who's considered the best carpet dealer in Agrabah. His name is Sharif."

"Let's take the Carpet to him right away,"

said Jasmine. "I'm ready to try anything."

Ten minutes later, Jasmine, Aladdin, and Abu left the palace by one of the side doors. Aladdin carried the rolled carpet under one arm and Abu on his shoulder.

"This way," said Aladdin. He took Jasmine's hand and they crossed into a narrow street that led to the marketplace.

Aladdin and Jasmine focused their attention on dodging people, carts, camels, and horses. Abu took in all the sights from Aladdin's shoulder. They passed close to a stall stacked high with shiny brass pots and lamps. Abu stretched out his arm.

"Keep those sticky fingers to yourself!" said Aladdin. "No more stealing. Remember?"

Abu shrugged and folded his arms across his chest. He then turned his attention to the crowd. Children chased each other around the stalls. A merchant shouted at a camel to move out of the middle of the street.

Two men dressed in Bedouin robes slipped in and out of view. Abu stood on Aladdin's shoulder to look at the men more closely. He shook his head and rocked from side to side.

"Sit still," said Aladdin. "You're making it hard for me to walk."

Abu chattered into Aladdin's ear.

"Why are you so nervous?" Aladdin asked.

Abu kept chattering.

"Relax," said Aladdin. "You're giving me a headache."

Abu chattered once more, but Aladdin ignored him. Abu rubbed his head and peered into the crowd.

"There's Sharif," Aladdin said. He pointed to a man near a stall stacked high with rugs. When they reached him, Aladdin asked, "May we speak with you alone for a moment?"

Sharif nodded and held back the heavy tapestry that closed off the stall. Jasmine, Aladdin, and Abu stepped inside.

"How may Sharif, the humble carpet dealer, serve you?" he asked in a deep voice.

Aladdin unrolled the Magic Carpet.

"Ah, lovely carpet!" said Sharif, caressing the intricate pattern. "Very old. And very valuable. I rarely see this kind of weaving—so complicated and yet so delicate. I hope you are interested in selling. I will pay you a handsome sum for this carpet. One thousand dinars!"

Aladdin shook his head. "We're not here to sell it. We'd just like some information."

"We're trying to find out more about the Carpet," said Jasmine. "We think a word that starts with the letters K, H, U, R might be important."

Sharif rubbed his chin and thought out loud. "K, H, U, R...khur...has something to do with a carpet..."

"Can you think of anything at all?" Aladdin asked.

Sharif seemed lost in thought. "Khuriya. Perhaps Khuriya."

"What's Khuriya?" Aladdin asked.

The carpet dealer shrugged. "Oh, it's probably nothing. Just a story my grandmother told me long ago. She said that the Great Eastern Desert was sometimes called The Place of Khuriya when she was very young. I mention it only because the towns there once produced the finest carpets. But all that was long before I was born."

"Did your grandmother tell you what 'Khuriya' meant?" asked Aladdin.

Sharif shook his head.

Jasmine and Aladdin asked Sharif a few more questions, but he couldn't give them any other clues. They thanked him for his help and left.

On their way back through the market, Aladdin noticed a display of melons. "Those are beauties," he said. "Let's buy some for the royal chef."

Just as Aladdin leaned the Carpet against the stall, Abu let out a screech. The canopy above the stall crashed down. It blanketed everyone and everything nearby.

"Jasmine!" cried Aladdin. "Abu!" He scrambled around as best he could under the heavy fabric to find them. People pushed and screamed. Aladdin felt arms flinging, hands grabbing, and legs kicking. There was shouting all around.

Finally the canopy was lifted. Aladdin saw Jasmine and Abu sitting on the ground nearby. He hugged them.

"You're all right!" he said. He brushed some dust off Abu's nose. Abu wiggled out of Aladdin's hands and pointed at two robed figures slinking away from the stall.

"Hey!" Aladdin said, looking at the ground. "The Carpet! Where is it?"

Aladdin began to search frantically. He combed through the melons, plums, and apples that had toppled off the stand.

"Have you seen a carpet?" he asked the vegetable seller. "A blue carpet with gold tassels? Please, have you seen one?"

The merchant shook his head. The Carpet had vanished.

CHAPTER 3

he last of the sun's rays danced in the reflecting pool in the palace courtyard. Three sad figures sat at the edge of the pool.

"I'll never look at another melon as long as I live," said Aladdin.

Abu sniffled twice. Jasmine handed him another handkerchief, then she jumped up.

"Let's stop moping around," she said. "We're going to find the Magic Carpet— even if it takes until the north wind blows south!"

"But where do we start?" asked Aladdin. "We don't have even one clue."

"Sure we do," answered Jasmine. "We

know that once upon a time the word 'Khuriya' had something to do with the Great Eastern Desert."

"That's a clue?" Aladdin threw up his hands. "What are we going to do? Cross a desert on camels, looking for a carpet? I won't do it! Never!"

The next morning found Aladdin, Jasmine, and Abu swaying along on their camels as they set out for the Great Eastern Desert.

"We have enough supplies for a month," said Jasmine, "so we can just relax and concentrate on finding the Carpet."

Aladdin looked around. Sand and dunes stretched as far as he could see. "It shouldn't be too hard to concentrate," he murmured. "Where's the first oasis?"

"About five days from here," said Jasmine.

For four days, the sun beat down on the caravan as it moved eastward. At night, cold winds blew, and the travelers huddled in thick blankets beneath the stars.

On the fifth day, Jasmine stared blankly at the horizon as her camel trudged on. "Now I understand why people see mirages in the desert," she said. "I'm so tired of sand, I'd like to see anything else. Right now, my eyes are pretending they see palm trees up ahead."

Aladdin squinted at the horizon. "I see palm trees, too!" he exclaimed. "Maybe it's not a mirage!"

An hour later, the dusty travelers were washing their faces and hands at the well in a small oasis. Abu dipped his tail in the water and sprinkled drops on top of his head.

"Shall I draw more water for your camels?" asked the young girl who worked at the well. Aladdin nodded and gave her a silver coin.

"Oh, thank you!" said the girl. She hurried over to the camels.

Jasmine watched her and whispered to Aladdin, "That girl looks so sad. How old could she be? Twelve or thirteen?"

"Spending all her time in a place like this can't be easy for a child," said Aladdin. "And I'm not sure it's going to be so great for us, either. Do you really think we'll find anything here?"

Jasmine looked around at the half-dozen small buildings that made up the oasis and, to the east, at the forbidding peaks of a barren mountain range.

"It's not very encouraging," she said. "It's like looking for one particular pebble in the biggest ocean. We might walk around this desert for a hundred years and never find out anything about the Carpet."

Abu scampered up to Aladdin and offered him a date from one of the trees. Aladdin shook his head. Abu offered the date to Jasmine. She, too, shook her head. Abu shrugged and bit into the date himself.

"Here's what I think," said Aladdin. He threw a stone against the side of the well. "Our luck could change anytime. When we least expect it, we might find the solution to the mystery staring us right in the face."

"And for now," added Jasmine, "we'll use the only clue we have—the word 'Khuriya.'"

Aladdin nodded. He tossed another stone

hard against the side of the well—and another. "Khuriya," he said. "What does it mean? Khuriya!"

Crash! Splash! Splash!

Aladdin spun around. The girl stood just a few feet away. Her eyes were as round as moons. Her hands shook. The two buckets of water she had been carrying lay overturned on the ground.

"You—you know about it," the girl whispered. Her voice trembled. "You know about Khuriya!"

CHAPTER 4

on't be frightened," Aladdin said gently. "We won't harm you. Something precious was stolen from us. We're trying to find it."

The girl stared at Aladdin, Jasmine, and Abu as if she were trying to decide whether to trust them. Then she took Jasmine's hand. "My name is Asha," she said. "Please come with me."

Asha led them to the smallest house in the oasis. It had only a single room. She closed the door and motioned her guests to sit on a straw mat.

Jasmine and Aladdin looked at each other. They had a hundred questions to ask Asha.

She made coffee and served it to them in small blue cups, then she sat on the mat facing them.

"I will tell you my story and the story of Khuriya," she began in a quiet voice.

Jasmine and Aladdin nodded. Abu crept closer.

"One thousand years ago, an old sorcerer lived in this very region. His name was Khuriya. He was a weaver by profession, and a few months before he died, he wove one hundred flying carpets. He gave each one a unique pattern and combination of colors. When he finished the weaving, Khuriya scattered the carpets over the desert and its cities and towns. 'Go!' he said. 'Find masters. Serve them well. And remember my name.'

"Hours before he died, Khuriya called for his helper, a boy named Asmar. 'I will now teach you the secret of the flying carpets,' the sorcerer said. 'You must do exactly as I say, or the carpets will lose their magic powers. When you are old, you must pass the secret on to your eldest child. When that child

grows old, the secret must be passed on again—and again and again.'

"'Each evening at sunset, you will weave a small square of cloth on this silver loom. Use threads of gold. You will weave the letters of my name, Khuriya, into the cloth. Then, at sunrise each morning, you will unravel the gold cloth, save the threads, and use them to reweave the cloth at sunset.'

"Khuriya, the sorcerer, died at noon. That evening at sunset, Asmar began his daily work of weaving and unraveling the golden cloth. Asmar kept his promise to Khuriya, and so did his eldest child, and so did the next child, and the next..."

Asha paused for a moment and looked up at Aladdin and Jasmine.

"And you," Aladdin asked quietly. "Are you a child of the children of Asmar?"

The girl nodded. "I am Asha Asmar. I share this home with my grandfather. About a month ago, he began to teach me how to weave the golden cloth on the silver loom. But then..." Asha hesitated. Her eyes filled with tears.

"Please," Aladdin said, patting her hand, "tell us what happened."

Asha took a deep breath. "A month ago, my grandfather was kidnapped in the middle of the night, and the silver loom was stolen!"

Tears fell down Asha's cheeks. Abu jumped up and offered her his crumpled handkerchief.

Jasmine sighed. "Really, Abu, I'll give her a fresh one."

While Asha dried her eyes, Aladdin told her the story of their carpet. "It makes perfect sense now," he said. "The Carpet began losing its powers about a month ago—just when your grandfather was kidnapped and stopped weaving the gold cloth!"

"Whoever kidnapped him," said Jasmine, "wants the secret of the magic carpets."

"And probably all the carpets, too," Aladdin added. "But our first job is to rescue your grandfather."

"Do you have any idea where he could have been taken?" asked Jasmine.

"I can only guess," said Asha. "There's an ancient castle high in the Eastern Mountains. Some people believe Khuriya once lived there. It would be the best hiding place in the region."

"Is it hard to get there?" Aladdin asked.

Asha nodded. "There's no road, and it's much too steep for camels. We'd have to walk, and that would take more than a week."

"Oh, no!" said Aladdin. "This is just when we need a magic carpet!"

"Or a genie," said Jasmine. She put her hands on her hips. "Where is that big blue bag of wind when we really need him?"

CHAPTER 5

Bang! Bang! Bang! Someone was pounding on the door.

"The kidnappers are back!" cried Asha.

Aladdin stood in front of the door with his fists clenched. "Who's there?" he called.

"Why, it's just little old me," said the Genie. He stepped through the door without opening it. He wore tennis clothes and was carrying a tennis racket. "My mama always told me to knock when I visit someone for the first time."

The Genie pulled off his sunglasses and looked around the room. He glared at Jasmine and Aladdin. "Is this your idea of a health spa, a place for recreation and healing, a place to get mind and body together?"

"Genie—" Jasmine began.

"What are you kids doing to yourselves?" the Genie continued. "No offense intended," he said to Asha, "but this place ain't the Alhambra. Just look at you guys. Skin like old leather. Hair like straw. Too much of that ultraviolet. Jasmine, honey, it's time for a facial. And you, dear—" he turned to Asha, "those red eyes! Now, hip hop! I have just five minutes before tennis. Get your jammies and we're off!"

"Genie!" said Aladdin. "We have serious business here. If Asha has red eyes, it's because she's been crying. Her grandfather was kid-napped, and—"

The Genie gasped. "Say no more. Poor little thing." He turned himself into a plump man with a lap as big as an armchair. "Come to Uncle Genie," he said, pulling Asha onto his lap. "Now tell me everything that happened."

It took only a few minutes for Asha to repeat the story.

"Gotcha," said the Genie. He changed back to his normal shape, flung open the door and stepped outside. "So now the job is for me to get us to this mountaintop castle?"

"Do you think you can do it?" asked Aladdin, following him out the door.

The Genie whirled around and scooped Aladdin up with one immense blue hand. "Is water wet? Do rotten eggs smell? Does soda pop come in cans? Get real, Laddie. I can do just about anything!" With that, the Genie put Aladdin down and stared out at the distant mountains.

The sun had set, and the desert was bathed in pale moonlight. The Genie glanced around the oasis and rolled his eyes. "Not exactly one of your top-ten air-transport hubs—but I'm never one to complain." He stood at attention, saluted sharply, and announced, "Welcome, scouts, to Middle-of-Nowhere International Airship Station!"

The air was filled with the noise of a

gigantic air pump. *Whoosh! Whoosh! Whoosh!*

"Look at that," Asha whispered.

"An even bigger blue windbag," said Jasmine.

The Genie was expanding into an airship. He grew fatter and fatter. He lifted off the ground and floated in the air horizontally. A passenger gondola appeared underneath the Genie. A propeller sprouted at one end and began to revolve. A carpet dropped down from the gondola.

The Genie's voice echoed across the desert. "Flight 007, royal-class service to Mountain Castle now boarding. Kiddies and dangerous pets can board first. Folks who get airsick should stay home. Remember—there are no overhead luggage compartments. Sharp objects are not allowed on board. And: I am not a blimp! Prepare for takeoff!"

Jasmine and Asha scrambled into their seats followed by Aladdin and Abu. As they were fastening their seatbelts, the carpet was pulled up, and the airship rose into the night

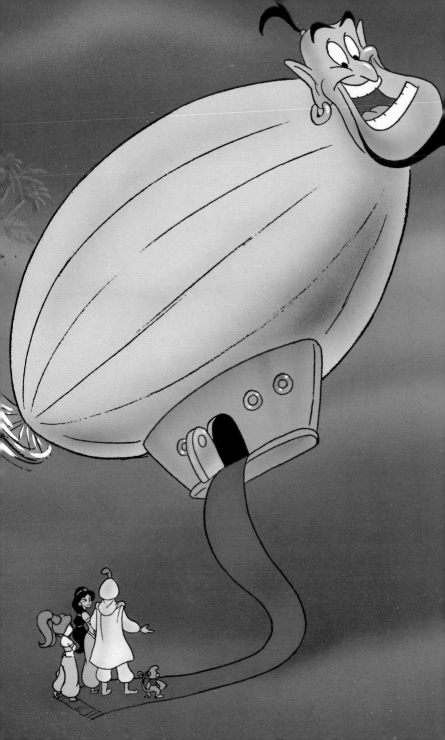

sky. It circled once over the oasis and then shot forward at full speed toward the mountains.

"Aren't we going awfully fast?" Asha asked. She looked out the window and turned pale.

"Don't worry," said Aladdin. "We've gone for lots of rides with this genie. He's always in full control."

The Genie's deep voice swept back to them. "Genie to control tower. Genie to control tower. There seems to be a loss of brake function at full throttle position while airborne. Do you read me? Please come in. Like, guys—I don't have a clue about stopping this thing!"

The mountaintop castle, with its tall watchtowers and balconies surrounded by low-walled parapets, came into view. It was directly ahead of them.

Asha grabbed Jasmine's arm, and Jasmine reached for Aladdin. Abu covered his eyes. Without slowing down, the airship whipped around a tower. Then it stopped short, and the red carpet flipped down like a stairway onto a parapet.

"Faked you out! Faked you out!" announced the Genie.

"Very funny," muttered Aladdin as he, Jasmine, and Asha hurried down the carpet stairs.

"Where's your sense of humor?" the Genie asked.

"Shhh," Jasmine whispered. "Do you want them to hear us?"

"Sorry." The Genie swirled back into his usual shape. "Guess I got carried away."

The group tiptoed across the balcony to a window.

"There he is!" Asha whispered. "Oh, my poor grandfather! We must save him!"

CHAPTER 6

laddin, Jasmine, Abu, and the Genie crowded around Asha and looked through the window. In a cavernous stone room, a frail old man sat hunched over a carpet. He was surrounded by a dozen guards in uniform. Next to him was a heap of wool.

"Whoops!" said the Genie. "I'm getting mucho bad vibes from those guards. They work for Al Ghanab, the cruelest thief in all the Great Eastern Desert. His men call him The Butcher."

"Can you see what your grandfather is doing?" Aladdin asked Asha.

"Yes," she answered. "Grandfather seems

to be unraveling a carpet."

Jasmine gasped. "That's our carpet!"

Asha pressed her face closer to the window. "Yours looks like the last one," she said.

"Genie, what do you think?" asked Aladdin.

The Genie said, "The little missy's right. They've made the old guy unravel all the other carpets from the looks of that pile of wool next to him."

"We need to find out what Al Ghanab is planning," said Aladdin. "I'll sneak inside and see if I can hear what they're saying."

"Not necessary, my boy," said the Genie. "I'll just set up a little A-G-E."

"What's 'A-G-E?'" asked Asha.

"Advanced Genie Eavesdropping." The Genie tipped his head toward the window. His ear stretched until it was gigantic in size. "Major gross," said the Genie, "but effective."

Abu, who was sitting on his shoulder, and also listening, nodded.

"Can you hear anything?" Aladdin asked.

The Genie nodded. "Well, how about that!

You don't say! Would you believe! Well, I never! Oh, puh-leeze!"

Aladdin shook the Genie's arm. "What's going on?"

The Genie pulled his ear away from the window. "Here's the scoop, guys. Al Ghanab and his goons snatched all one hundred magic carpets and made Grandpops turn them into string. Now Grandpops is getting orders to weave the stuff into a mega-carpet, big enough to hoist an army. Al Ghanab figures that with the supercarpet he'll be able to defeat every sultan around and rule Agrabah and all the other kingdoms. Gramps says he won't do the weaving, and so Al Ghanab is going to—" The Genie drew one finger slowly across his throat.

"They're going to kill him!" cried Asha.

"Murderers!" said Aladdin. He began to pace. "We have to get rid of the guards."

"I'll do it! I'll do it!" chirped the Genie, waving his hand in the air. "Pick me, teacher! I'm the best! I'll blast them away with a cannon. I'll set the place on fire. I'll bring in a tidal wave! I'll—"

Jasmine shook her head. "I have a better idea—one that will keep Grandfather Asmar safe. We'll use music!"

"Music?" asked Asha.

"Yes," said Jasmine. "We'll hide on the balcony. Then Aladdin will play the flute and I'll sing. The guards will come out to investigate—and the Genie will take care of things from there!"

"Sounds good to me," said Aladdin.

The Genie whirled and put his face up against Aladdin's. "Are you nutso in the head or what?" he snapped. "We're not playing with Little Bunny Foo-Foo today. This guy is Attila the Hun, Genghis Khan, and the Abominable Snowman all rolled into one. And she's going to *sing?*"

Jasmine put a hand on the Genie's arm. "Trust me," she whispered.

"'Trust me,' she says. 'Okay, okay.'"

The Genie handed Aladdin a flute and disappeared. Everyone else hid in the shadows. Aladdin began playing the flute. Jasmine sang a haunting melody—low but piercing.

The heavy iron door to the stone room swung open. "Who goes there?" bellowed one of the guards. "Show yourself right now, or I'll chop your head off!"

The guard stepped onto the balcony. Aladdin and Jasmine kept up their song. Two more guards stepped out. Then four, six, and nine more. The music continued.

The guards milled around the balcony and peered over the parapet wall. A distant rumbling grew louder and drowned out the music. The mountain began to quake. A high-speed train zoomed over the desert toward the castle.

The guards froze. The train rose into the air and screeched to a halt alongside the parapet wall. When the doors opened, the Genie popped out. He was wearing a conductor's uniform.

"This is an express train making no stops!" he shouted. "Stand clear of the closing doors!"

With one hand, the Genie swept the

guards into the train. The doors snapped shut. Then he jabbed his finger into the side of the mountain and hollowed out a tunnel. The train raced into the tunnel. The Genie stood on the rear platform and waved.

"We did it!" shouted Aladdin. "We won!"

A deep voice behind him growled, "That's what you think."

Aladdin spun around. A man with narrow, glinting eyes was looming over him. He pointed a long sword at Aladdin's throat.

"The Butcher!" gasped Aladdin.

"You've been meddling in my affairs, and I don't like meddlers," Al Ghanab snarled. He took a step toward Aladdin.

Aladdin began inching back toward the parapet wall. Al Ghanab pressed forward. They moved step by step. Aladdin kept both eyes on Al Ghanab and one hand behind his back. When his fingertips touched the cold parapet wall, he felt for a loose rock and found one. He raised his hand to throw.

"Fool!" shouted Al Ghanab. He swung his

sword and knocked the stone from Aladdin's hand. Then he raised his sword higher and roared, "I kill meddlers!"

CHAPTER 7

s Aladdin ducked to the side, Abu dashed between Al Ghanab's legs. Tripping over Abu, the thief swung wide with his sword. It slammed into the parapet wall and broke. With Abu tangled in his legs, Al Ghanab couldn't regain balance. He stumbled forward against the wall.

"Nice work, Abu!" said Aladdin. Using all his strength, he lifted Al Ghanab's legs and flipped him over the wall.

"Over you go!" Aladdin shouted. Al Ghanab screamed as he hurtled down.

The train shot out of the tunnel in reverse. Still standing on the rear platform, the Genie stretched out an arm and caught Al Ghanab.

"I knew one little lamb had strayed," he said. "Naughty, naughty!" The Genie waved at Aladdin. The train disappeared into the tunnel again.

"Grandfather!" Asha called. She ran into the castle and threw her arms around him. He seemed stunned. His eyes grew moist.

Grandfather Asmar's voice was barely more than a whisper. "Asha, my child. I feared I would never see you again! Ah, Asha, such evil plans were in the mind of Al Ghanab."

"We're safe now, Grandfather," said Asha. "My new friends have gotten rid of him."

Grandfather Asmar held out a thin hand to Aladdin and Jasmine. His smile showed relief and gratitude.

"Where's Abu?" Aladdin suddenly asked. He glanced around the room. "Abu?"

Angry chattering came from the pile of tangled wool on the floor. Then Abu appeared, dragging what remained of Aladdin's Magic Carpet.

Abu stopped chattering. He held the Carpet up to his cheek and wiped his tears.

"Not on the Carpet!" Jasmine exclaimed.

"Ah, yes," Grandfather Asmar sighed. "The magic carpets. What a loss to the world!"

"What do you mean?" asked Aladdin. "Can't they be rewoven? All the wool is right here."

Grandfather Asmar shook his head. "Khuriya wove the carpets in unique patterns. He wove them to hold a magic spell and to last forever. It would take a weaver like me a year to redo each carpet. A century to restore all one hundred of them."

"A century!" said Jasmine.

"Shouldn't we at least begin?" asked Aladdin. "It would be better than doing nothing."

Grandfather Asmar looked down at his hands. "I shall never weave again," he said. "When the guards forced me to rip apart the carpets, not only was my heart broken, my hands were also ruined. I can barely move them now."

"Is there nothing we can do?" asked Asha.

Her grandfather shook his head. "I'm afraid we would need powerful magic."

"Powerful magic?" Jasmine looked toward the door. "Where is that genie now?"

Silence. Abu began chattering again and pointed to a corner of the room. The Genie was stretched out on the floor, doing sit-ups.

"Geeeenie..." Jasmine began.

The Genie turned purple and held up both hands. "No way, José! Don't even think about it. This genie does not do carpets. Nosiree!"

He blew up to twice his normal size. "Now, listen up!" he thundered. "I do earthquakes, volcanoes, monsoons, hurricanes, frog infestations, and major flooding. But no carpets!"

"Geeeenie..." said Aladdin.

"Come on, Al," the Genie pleaded. He nodded toward Grandfather Asmar. "No disrespect to Pops over there, but do I look like a weaver? Let's get serious. Weavers have those itsy-bitsy, teeny-weeny, nimble little fingers. Guys, I'm telling you—I'm all thumbs!"

The Genie held up two gigantic hands— that were all thumbs.

Aladdin shrugged. "Okay, so you're not powerful enough. Maybe we can find another genie to help us..."

"Not powerful enough? You'll find another genie, will you?" The Genie stuck his tongue out at Aladdin and sat down cross-legged in front of Grandfather Asmar. "Show me your stuff, Gramps," he said.

Grandfather Asmar asked that the wooden loom on the other side of the room be brought to him. Then he took the Magic Carpet from Abu. "First, I'll show you the basic patterns," he said to the Genie.

A half-hour later, the Genie stood up. "I think I've got the basics, Gramps. You can fill in the fine points along the way."

"How long will it take?" Aladdin asked.

The Genie rolled his eyes and sighed. "My, aren't we pushy today!" Then he snapped his fingers. "Gimme an order for a hundred car-

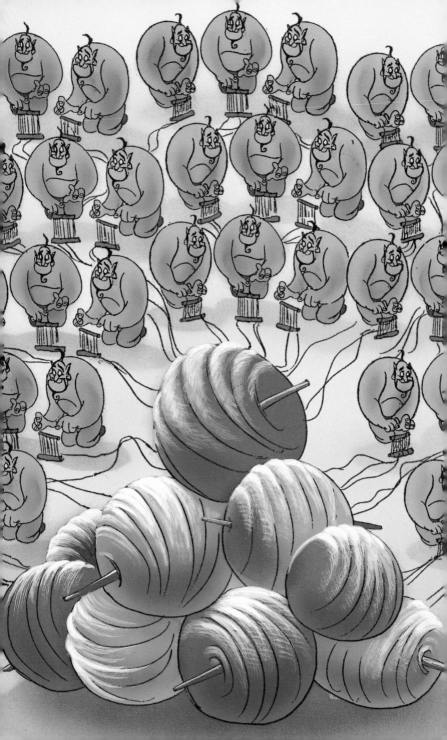

pets, and I'll get myself a hundred weavers. They don't call me Señor Smarts for nothing!"

The Genie snapped his fingers again—and turned himself into one hundred little genies, each sitting in front of a loom.

"Ready...get set...GO!" shouted the genies in unison. A blur of arms and hands rushed back and forth across the looms. Wood slats clattered. Wool threads flew through the air. The little genies bent over their work, all humming noisily.

Grandfather Asmar, supported by Asha, moved from one loom to the next. He examined the weaving carefully. "Good work," he said.

"What'd you expect?" muttered the genies.

The genies worked all night and through the next afternoon. Finally they got up from their looms. One hundred exquisite carpets lay neatly on the floor. One little genie snapped its fingers. They all disappeared. Strutting across the room in their place was the big blue Genie.

"You're marvelous!" said Jasmine.

"The greatest!" said Aladdin. "Shall we try the carpets out?" He stood in front of his own carpet and commanded, "Fly, Carpet!"

The Carpet didn't move.

CHAPTER 8

hat's going on?" asked Aladdin. He tried again, "Carpet, please fly!"

The Carpet didn't budge. Not even a tassel fluttered.

The Genie looked horrified. "I've failed!" he whispered. "My magic has failed!" He melted himself into a large blue puddle. "I'm all washed up. Finished. Wrecked. Ruined. Kaput."

"What happened?" Asha asked. "Is there something wrong with the weaving?"

"Oh, no," Grandfather Asmar answered. "The weaving is fine. But the carpets won't fly until the name of the sorcerer Khuriya is woven into the golden cloth at sunset. This must be done in order to recast and maintain the magic spell."

The Genie sprang out of the blue puddle. "Why didn't you say so? No problem, man. Just give me the gold stuff, and we're back in business."

"I'm afraid that's not possible," said Grandfather. "Only an Asmar can weave the golden cloth and restore the magic of Khuriya."

"What is this?" the Genie demanded. "Anti-genie discrimination? I'll call my lawyer! I'll organize a protest march. I'll—"

All eyes turned to Asha Asmar.

"I-I can't! I'm too young. I haven't finished my training. I..." Asha paused and looked from Aladdin to Abu and then from Jasmine to her grandfather. She took a deep breath and held out her hand.

Her grandfather in turn held out his hand. On his palm lay a spool of gold thread. "Use my loom," he said. He pointed to the silver loom.

Asha took the thread and walked over to

the loom. The sky had turned a brilliant pattern of orange, violet, and pale green. Only a sliver of the sun's red disk remained above the horizon. With the loom, Asha sat down at the window. Slowly and carefully she began to weave.

No one spoke—except the Genie. "Isn't that sweet?" he blubbered, wiping away a tear. "Another little weaver. I just love weavers."

As the last colors of the sunset faded, Asha stood up. She carried a small square of gold cloth to her grandfather. He studied it. Then he held it up for everyone to see. In the center of the cloth, Asha had woven a delicate pattern of letters. They spelled "Khuriya."

Smiling, Asha's grandfather waved his hand gently, just once.

The one hundred carpets began to stir. Their edges rippled. Their tassels fluttered. Slowly one lifted itself off the floor. Then another...and another. Soon the vast stone room was filled with hovering carpets—one hundred jewel-like carpets—as lovely as a flock of the rarest birds.

"It's time to say good-bye," murmured Grandfather Asmar. He looked at the carpets. "I wonder if we might get a ride home."

A blue and gold carpet with purple tassels swooped slowly across the room. It stopped in front of Asha and her grandfather.

"It's time for all the carpets to fly back to their owners," said Jasmine.

"And time for us to go home, too," said Aladdin. Then he, Jasmine, and Abu hugged both the Asmars.

"Well? Are you just going to stand there?" Aladdin asked the Genie.

The Genie tapped his foot impatiently on the floor. "Look, folks, I don't mean to sound like a broken record—but after what you've been through, I have only two words to say: health spa."

A second later, the Genie was dressed in his workout clothes. "Last chance—and you'd better join up, guys. I mean—just get a load of Gramps over here. A little jogging, a nice massage, some customized workouts—he'll be weaving like a maniac in no time. Whataya say, campers? Huh? Huh? Huh?"

Aladdin shook his head.

"Maybe some other time," said Grandfather Asmar.

"Oh, phooey," said the Genie.

Asha and her grandfather settled themselves and the silver loom onto a carpet. Aladdin, Jasmine, and Abu climbed onto their carpet. Its tassels flipped and flapped for joy.

"I might as well fly with you part of the way," said the Genie.

One by one, all the carpets glided through the castle door, over the parapet wall, and out over the open desert. One hundred carpets dipped and soared and sailed through the clear evening sky. Soon they were small specks on the horizon, and only a distant voice echoed back across the sand dunes.

"I'm telling you—they've got mud baths like you've never seen..."